paperthorn tree
hyena
D1415846
dark wild wood
guineafowl grassland
big fig tree
coral tree
crocodile river
cabbage tree
mud bath
tortoise flats

For my parents

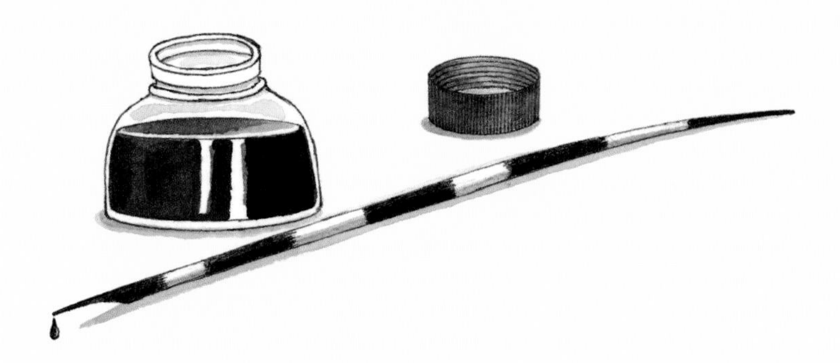

First published in Great Britain in 2007 and in the USA in 2008 by
Frances Lincoln Children's Books, 4 Torriano Mews,
Torriano Avenue, London NW5 2RZ
www.franceslincoln.com

Distributed in the USA by Publishers Group West

British Library Cataloguing in Publication Data available on request

ISBN: 978-1-84507-587-3

The illustrations for this book are watercolour.

Printed in Singapore
1 3 5 7 9 8 6 4 2

Noko's Surprise Party

Fiona Moodie

F
FRANCES LINCOLN
CHILDREN'S BOOKS

Takadu the aardvark and Noko the porcupine were old friends. They lived in a little house at the foot of the Mbombo hills.

Takadu got up one morning very, very early. He wrote out five invitations. One each for Mrs Warthog, Bat-eared Fox, Pangolin, Vervet Monkey and Guineafowl. It took him quite a long time.

Surprise birthday party for:
Noko
When: tomorrow
Where: at home
There will be FIGS!
Please Come
Love Takadu

Greedy Hyena was not invited to the party. His manners were too terrible. But he watched Takadu deliver the invitations.

"I'll show that mean Takadu," he muttered.

When Takadu had given out the invitations, he walked all the way to the Big Fig Tree. He picked figs until the sun was high in the sky. It was hard work but he didn't mind because they were for Noko's party.

Takadu filled his basket to the brim, tied it on to his back and set off on the long journey home.

He had to go through the Dark Wild Wood on the way and he couldn't help shivering.

As he crept through the wood, Takadu sang a song to keep the bats out of his ears.

"Bats be gone!
Bats behave!
Here comes Takadu the Brave!"

Takadu heard a little squeak coming from one of the trees. It was Bushbaby.

"Oh, I'm so HUNGRY and I can't find ANYTHING to eat," she snuffled. "I've eaten nothing but horrible tree ants for DAYS."

"I've got plenty of figs," said Takadu. "Here you are." And he gave Bushbaby a juicy fig.

Bushbaby jumped up and down on her branch for joy.

"Thank you, Takadu! You are so kind."

Takadu added a verse to his song as he walked on:

> "If you're hungry, if you're cold,
> Come to Takadu the Bold."

He was glad to leave the Dark Wild Wood,
and his basket seemed a little lighter to carry.

In the grass ahead of him, four scaly little legs were waving around. It was poor old Mountain Tortoise, upside down.

"I was climbing that ant-heap," sobbed Tortoise, "and I slipped and fell on my back and I've been lying here all day in the hot sun. I think I'm going to die of thirst!"

“You’re not going to die,” said Takadu cheerfully, as he turned old Mountain Tortoise the right way up. “This will make you feel better.” And he carefully put a fig in front of Tortoise.

“Thank you, thank you,” cried Tortoise, as the fig juice ran down his chin.

Takadu walked along in the hot sun. Now his basket was even lighter to carry, but the sun was very hot. He began to feel tired.

"I'll just lie down under this cabbage tree for a nap," he said to himself. He curled up in the shade and soon he was fast asleep.

All this time, Greedy Hyena had been watching and waiting.

"Ha!" he growled. "I'll teach Takadu not to ask me to his party! Now's my chance!"

Hyena crept up and gobbled up all the figs that were left in the basket. He left just one, to tease Takadu.

When Takadu woke up, the sun was very low in the sky and his basket was empty, except for one fig and a strong smell of Hyena.

All that work for nothing! Takadu was cross and sad. No figs! Noko's birthday would be ruined.

Sneaky Hyena rolled on his back behind a rock and laughed till he cried.

"Oh well," Takadu sighed. "I'll have to think of another present for Noko." Takadu thought and thought, and at last he gave a little jump for joy.

"That's it!" he cried. "I'll make up a birthday song!"

And all the way back, that's what he did.

The next day was Noko's birthday. After breakfast, Takadu fetched his guitar.

"Happy birthday, Noko," he said. "This is for you.

A song of praise I sing today!
A birthday song I sing today!
For Noko who is good and kind.
A friend like Noko's hard to find.
In North or South or East or West,
Noko the porcupine is the Best, the Best, the Best!"

"Well, thank you very much," said Noko.

"Wait – it's not over yet," said Takadu.

"My birthday gift is not so big,
In fact, my friend, it's just one fig."

"Oh Takadu, it's the thought that counts," chuckled Noko.

Just then there was a loud knock at the door. Noko ran to open it.

"surprise!"

cried the five friends standing outside with their birthday gifts. Mrs Warthog had woven a banana leaf hat for Noko, Bat-eared Fox had brought a calabash of marula berry juice, Pangolin carried a basket of tasty roots, Vervet Monkey's gift was a length of liana rope (always useful),

and Guineafowl gave Noko a bowl of eggs (hard boiled).

"We've come to the fig party!" the friends chorused.

"But there ARE no figs," mumbled Takadu, scratching his ears and blushing.

And he told them what had happened.

"I know!" said Noko. "If the figs can't come to us, why don't we go to the figs?"

"Hurray!" the others shouted. "Let's have a fig picnic!" And off they went.

Bushbaby and old Mountain Tortoise joined them on the way. Bushbaby said she would sit in the fig tree and throw down figs because Takadu had been so kind to her. Old Tortoise said that anybody could use him for a headrest if they felt sleepy.

When they reached the Big Fig Tree, Noko and Takadu used the liana rope to make a water-slide over the river.

Bushbaby threw down figs and everybody ate and drank and swam and played all day long.

The only one who wasn't having fun was Hyena.
He watched the others from behind the coral tree
and felt very left out and grumpy.

But Noko wanted everyone to be happy on his birthday.

"Why don't you come and join in?" he called to Hyena. So Hyena did some juggling tricks with figs and soon they were all laughing together like old friends.

It was the best birthday party ever!

Mbombo hills
Takadu and Noko live here
flat rocks
big rocks
bathing pool
hippo path
crocodile river
pangolin place
monkey
palm
bat-eared fox
hole